BOING
BOING

To Lottie Boss

Published in 2021 in Great Britain by
Barrington Stoke Ltd
18 Walker Street, Edinburgh, EH3 7LP

www.barringtonstoke.co.uk

This edition based on *Boing Boing*
(Barrington Stoke, 2016)

Text © 1992 & 2021 Alexander McCall Smith
Illustrations © 2016 Zoe Persico

A CIP catalogue record for this book is available
from the British Library upon request

ISBN: 978-1-80090-076-9

Printed by Hussar Books, Poland

Barrington Stoke

BOING BOING

ALEXANDER McCALL SMITH

ILLUSTRATED BY
ZOE PERSICO

There was something odd about Jane.

When she was a baby, she crawled.

But when she grew bigger, she ... bounced!

Everybody was astonished. One moment Jane was on one side of the room – then she was on the other.

"Did you see that?" asked her mother.

"Yes," said her father. "I think she bounced!"

Over the next days they watched Jane closely.

They watched Jane bounce out of bed and into the bathroom.

They watched her bounce downstairs and into the garden.

Everywhere she went, she bounced like a ball.

Jane's mother and father took her to the doctor. The doctor took an X-ray of Jane's legs.

"Look!" the doctor said. "She has springs in her knees!"

As Jane grew older, her bounces grew higher and higher.

At school Jane won all the high jump competitions.

She did very well at other games too.

Deep snow was no problem ...

And she could always get library books from the top shelves.

Bouncing was very useful, and people called her Springy Jane!

Then one day there was a terrible storm.

The flood water rose right up to the windows of an old lady's house. She had to climb onto the roof. No one could help her get down.

Then somebody said, "Call Springy Jane!"

With one bounce, Jane landed on the roof.
She picked up the old lady and bounced
down again, right over the water.

Everybody cheered!

Then, soaking wet, Jane bounced home and changed her clothes.

The next morning Jane was stiff. It was hard to bounce.

Her parents took her back to the doctor, who looked at Jane's knees and shook his head.

"I'm sorry," he said. "Your springs got rusty in the rain. I'll have to take them out."

Now Jane couldn't bounce. But she wasn't sad. It was fun to walk like everybody else.

And people still called her Springy Jane.

Jane liked that.

As for the old lady ... She made Jane a special birthday cake to say thank you.

There was something odd about the cake. Instead of candles, the cake had icing sugar springs!

There was a present too – a great big
metal spring.

"Oh good!" said Jane. "I can bounce again."

And she did.